A Note to Parents

DK READERS is a compelling program for beginning readers, designed in conjunction with leading literacy experts, including Dr. Linda Gambrell, Distinguished Professor of Education at Clemson University. Dr. Gambrelll has served as President of the National Reading Conference, the College Reading Association, and International Reading Association.

Beautiful illustrations and superb full-color photographs combine with engaging, easy-to-read stories and informational texts to offer a fresh approach to each subject in the series. Each DK READER is guaranteed to capture a child's interest while developing his or her reading skills, general knowledge, and love of reading.

The five levels of DK READERS are aimed at different reading abilities, enabling you to choose the books that are exactly right for your child:

Pre-level 1: Learning to read

Level 1: Beginning to read

Level 2: Beginning to read alone

Level 3: Reading alone

Level 4: Proficient readers

The "normal" age at which a child begins to read can be anywhere from three to eight years old. Adult participation through the lower levels is very helpful for providing encouragement, discussing storylines, and sounding out unfamiliar words.

No matter which level you select, you can be sure that you are helping your child learn to read, then read to learn!

DK

LONDON, NEW YORK,
MELBOURNE, MUNICH, AND DELHI

Project Editor Amy Junor
Designer Mark Richards
Brand Manager Lisa Lanzarini
Publishing Manager Simon Beecroft
Category Publisher Alex Allan
Production Controller Nick Seston
Production Editor Siu Chan

Reading Consultant
Linda B. Gambrell, Ph.D.

First published in the United States in 2008
by DK Publishing,
375 Hudson Street
New York, New York 10014

10 11 10 9 8 7 6 5 4

PD237—4/08

DK books are available at special discounts when purchased in bulk
for sales promotions, premiums, fund-raising, or educational use. For
details, contact:
DK Special Markets
375 Hudson Street, New York, New York 10014
SpecialSales@dk.com

A catalog record for this book is available from the Library of Congress.

ISBN: 978-0-7566-3488-9 (Paperback)
ISBN: 978-0-7566-3489-6 (Hardback)

Color reproduction by MDP, UK
Printed and bound in China by L Rex Printing Co., Ltd.

Discover more at

www.dk.com

DK READERS

Power Rangers Jungle Fury

We Are the Power Rangers

Written by Amy Junor

BEGINNING
1
TO READ

DK

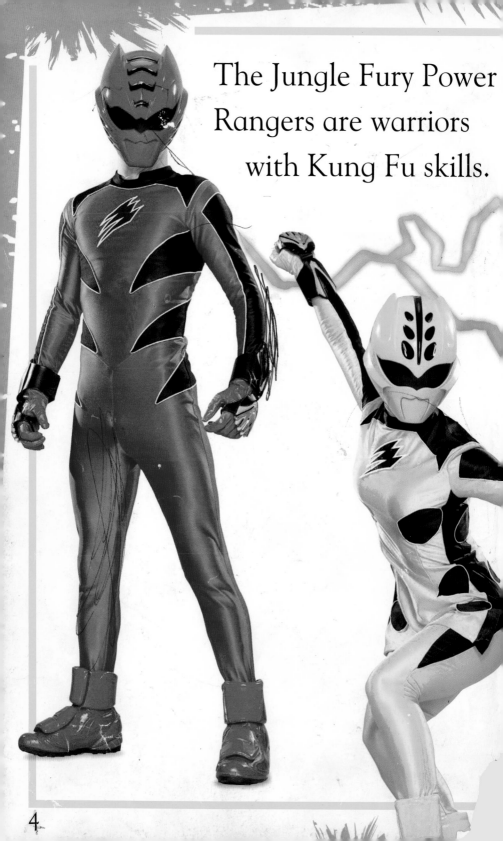

The Jungle Fury Power
Rangers are warriors
with Kung Fu skills.

They protect the Earth from an evil spirit called Dai Shi. Each Jungle Fury Power Ranger fights using the special powers of a wild animal.

Casey is the Red Ranger. He is the leader of the Power Rangers. Casey fights with the power of a tiger.

Like a tiger, Casey is tough and strong. He is also a fierce fighter.

tiger

The Red Ranger wears a special red helmet. His helmet covers his face. It protects his face in battle.

helmet

Theo Martin is
the Blue Power
Ranger.

Theo always tries to follow the rules. He likes to stay out of trouble. But he is on the same team as the rebel Casey, so it is hard to avoid trouble!

Theo fights with the power of a
jaguar. Jaguars are clever, fast
fighters, just like Theo.
When he is fighting, Theo moves
quickly and smoothly like a jaguar.

jaguar

13

Lily Chilman is the Yellow Power Ranger. She was captain of the cheer squad at her school. She is also a tough fighter.

Lily fights with the power of
the cheetah. Like a cheetah,
Lily is calm in battle,
with lightning-fast moves.

cheetah

Robert James
is known as RJ.
He is the Violet Power
Ranger. He is also
a Kung Fu Master.

RJ trains the other Power
Rangers. He fights with
the power of the wolf.

wolf

RJ first started learning Kung Fu
when he was a young boy.
He has been training all his life.

Now he has a lot to teach
the other Power Rangers!

Power Rangers ride into battle
on powerful robot vehicles
called zords.

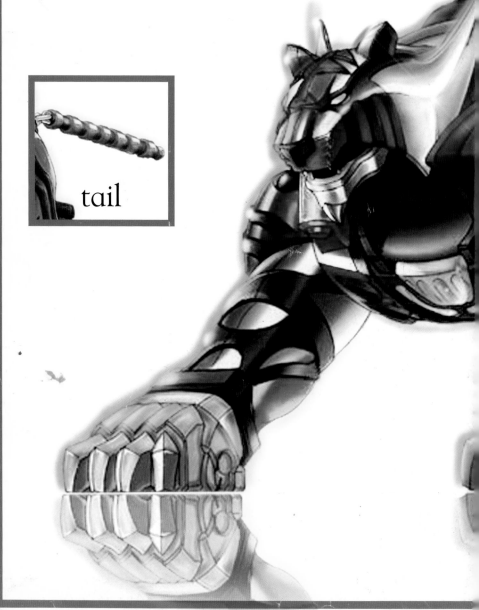

tail

Casey's zord looks like a tiger with a stripy tail.

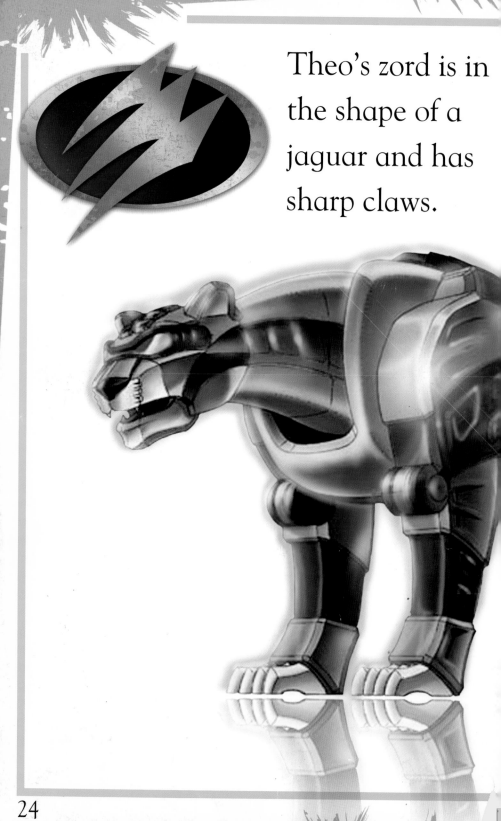

Theo's zord is in the shape of a jaguar and has sharp claws.

Jaguars are one of the fastest animals on Earth. The Blue Ranger's zord is one of the fastest vehicles.

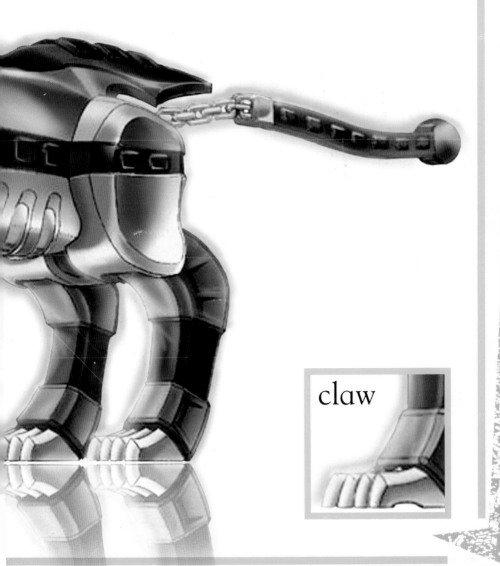

claw

A group of Kung Fu warriors called the Order of the Claw locked the evil spirit of Dai Shi in a special box.

When Dai Shi escaped, the Power Rangers had to save the world.

The Red Ranger
called his zord to help
him battle Dai Shi.
The evil spirit
was very strong.

Casey needed the help of his zord and all the other Rangers to beat Dai Shi.

The Power Rangers combined their zords to make a big, powerful Megazord.

Nothing can defeat a Megazord!

The Megazord defeated Dai Shi and the world was saved.

Picture word list

tiger
page 7

wolf
page 19

helmet
page 8

tail
page 22

jaguar
page 13

claw
page 25

cheetah
page 16